in Peril

Peter Clover

To Ann and Freddy

PUFFIN BOOKS

Published by the Penguin Group
Penguin Books Ltd, 27 Wrights Lane, London W8 5TZ, England
Penguin Putnam Inc., 375 Hudson Street, New York, New York 10014, USA
Penguin Books Australia Ltd, Ringwood, Victoria, Australia
Penguin Books Canada Ltd, 10 Alcorn Avenue, Toronto, Ontario, Canada M4V 3B2
Penguin Books (NZ) Ltd, Private Bag 102902, NSMC, Auckland, New Zealand

On the World Wide Web at: www.penguin.com

Penguin Books Ltd, Registered Offices: Harmondsworth, Middlesex, England

First published 2000
1 3 5 7 9 10 8 6 4 2

Sheltie is a trademark owned by Working Partners Ltd
Copyright © Peter Clover/Working Partners Ltd, 2000
All rights reserved

Created by Working Partners Ltd, London, W6 0QT

The moral right of the author has been asserted

Set in 14/22 Palatino

Made and printed in England by Clays Ltd, St Ives plc

British Library Cataloguing in Publication Data
A CIP catalogue record for this book is available from the British Library

ISBN 0–141–30455–3

Chapter One

'It won't be the same without you, Sally,' said Emma. 'But Sheltie and I will try and think up lots of things for us to do when you come back.'

Emma said goodbye to her best friend, then put down the telephone receiver. Sally was off to Scotland for four weeks to visit her auntie in Aberdeen. And that meant that

Emma would be spending the first four weeks of the summer holidays alone. Well, not completely alone. Emma always had Sheltie the little Shetland pony for company.

At just that moment, out in the paddock, Sheltie tossed back his head and called to Emma with a loud whinny. It was so loud that it almost rattled the cottage windows.

Emma smiled to herself as she hurried outside.

'OK, Sheltie. I'm coming!' she called.

Emma ran down the garden path to give Sheltie's ears a good hard scratch. Sheltie loved having his ears scratched. In fact, he loved having his chin scratched, his back scratched, his rump, and a spot behind his knees scratched as well! But ears were always his favourite.

Emma liked scratching his ears best of all too, because it made Sheltie close his eyes. And when he closed his eyes, the sunlight caught his long eyelashes and made them shine like gold.

'Here I am!' said Emma as she swung her legs over the top rail of the fence and dropped down into the paddock.

Sheltie blew her a wet raspberry and pushed his muzzle into Emma's arms for a hug.

'You big softie,' whispered Emma.

But Sheltie didn't seem to care. He liked getting cuddles as much as Emma liked giving them.

Later that morning, after a long grooming session, Emma tacked up

Sheltie, ready for a ride. The little pony's mane was brushed out into a silky waterfall and his tail billowed out, almost touching the floor. For once, Sheltie looked like a smart show pony.

'But I don't expect you'll stay like that for long!' said Emma. Emma knew that at the first opportunity, Sheltie would be rolling in the mud. He wasn't the kind of pony to stand still and look nice. Sheltie was mischievous and had a nose for adventure.

Emma tightened the girth strap and climbed up into the saddle. Then she fiddled with her stirrups.

'I think my legs have grown!' she

told Sheltie. The little pony flicked his head and gave a soft belch.

'And *you're* getting too fat. I think I'm going to put you on a diet before Sally gets back. I'll have you looking like one of those slim racehorses by the end of the holidays.'

Sheltie shook his mane and hiccuped. He didn't seem to like the idea of being put on a diet. He liked being round and plump.

But Emma was only joking. She really preferred him that way too.

'Walk on,' said Emma. 'We'll go somewhere different today. Somewhere we've never been before.'

But as Sheltie stood in the middle of the lane, Emma couldn't make up her mind about which way to ride.

'Go on, Sheltie,' she said. 'You choose!'

The little pony sniffed the air. Then he pricked up his ears before looking first left, then right.

Emma waited for Sheltie to decide which direction he wanted to go in. Then, when he seemed to have chosen, she flicked the reins loosely and encouraged him onwards.

Sheltie picked his way across the fields behind Horseshoe Pond, and headed off across the downs towards the moors. A high ridge separated the downs from the moorlands, and a bridle path ran along its length.

Normally, Emma and Sheltie

crossed the ridge and stepped over
on to the moor. But today, Sheltie
chose to turn left, past Mrs Warner's
cottage, and to walk along the bridle
path, away from Little Applewood.

Emma had never ridden Sheltie

this way before. But it was a lovely, sunny day and Mum had packed her sandwiches and a can of drink. Emma thought it was great fun letting Sheltie take her for a walk and she was enjoying every minute of the mystery ride.

Sheltie bounced along with an easy stride. He flicked his tail and took in the smells of the surrounding countryside.

Suddenly, up ahead, they saw another rider. Emma smiled to herself. It was always nice to meet other people out with their ponies. She recognized most of the ponies and riders in the area around Little Applewood. And this pair looked very familiar, although at first Emma couldn't quite tell who it was.

Then suddenly, Emma recognized both the rider and the pony. It was Melody Parker with her pony, Sapphire.

'Oh no!' groaned Emma.

Emma didn't like Melody Parker. In fact, none of her friends did either. Melody was a spoilsport and a troublemaker. If ever there was trouble, then Melody Parker would be the one to stir it up.

Emma took a deep breath and pulled in the reins. Sheltie recognized Melody and Sapphire too, and stamped his feet hard.

Emma felt her face going red and

she expected Melody to say something nasty as they passed. But to Emma's surprise, she didn't.

Melody managed a smile and said, 'Good morning, Emma. We don't often see you and Sheltie out here on the East Riding!'

Emma said, 'Hello,' but she was too surprised to say anything else. Then she flicked her heels and pushed Sheltie into a trot.

'Come on, boy. Just keep going. Don't look back,' she whispered. The thought of Melody Parker being friendly made Emma very suspicious indeed.

Chapter Two

Sheltie trotted forward with his ears flat against his head. The scent of Melody and her pony, Sapphire, was still fresh in his nostrils.

The little pony headed off down the winding bridle path that snaked its way across the Riding. They weren't very far out of Little Applewood, but everything looked different and new.

Emma glanced over her shoulder and saw Melody and Sapphire slip behind a wild copse of hawthorns.

'I wonder why Melody is suddenly being nice,' said Emma. 'Perhaps she

wants to be friends after all.' But the new countryside was so exciting that Emma didn't think about Melody for very long.

Up ahead, the bridle path opened out on to a green, grassy plain with rolling hills and sweeping carpets of heather.

In the distance, a clump of trees stood on top of a small hill. Sheltie jangled his reins and then looked towards the trees. He put on a spurt and began to canter along, with the breeze blowing through his mane.

But before they got to the trees, Emma noticed something else. At the foot of the hill, the ground sloped away into a shallow basin. And

nestling in the scooped-out basin was
a tumbledown cottage.

The roof of the building was
missing and some of the walls had
crumbled away. Green ivy grew up
and over the timbers making the
cottage quite difficult to see against
the grassy background.

'Now *that* would make a perfect
summer hideout,' murmured Emma.
Sheltie curled back his lips and blew
a soft whicker.

'It's almost invisible until you get
really close to it,' said Emma
enthusiastically. 'I wonder how many
people know it's here?'

Sheltie shook out his mane and
scraped at the grass with his hoof.

'Shall we go and investigate, boy?'

Emma didn't need to ask twice. The little pony pranced forward and picked his way carefully down the shallow slope. Emma leaned back in the saddle to make it easier for Sheltie to keep his footing. But as soon as he reached the bottom, Sheltie stepped sideways, away from the cottage.

'It's all right,' said Emma. She thought Sheltie seemed a little bit nervous, and clapped his neck hard to reassure him that everything was OK.

Sheltie made a grunting noise in the back of his throat, then inched his

way forward, towards the ivy-
covered ruin.

Emma spoke gently to Sheltie, but
his ears stayed flat against his head.

There was something about the tumbledown cottage that Sheltie wasn't happy about.

'I'll tell you what,' said Emma. 'You stay here and I'll go and look around, to make sure it's safe.'

Sheltie blew a thundering snort. He didn't seem to like *that* idea either.

'Don't worry, boy,' soothed Emma. 'I'll be extra careful.'

She loosely tethered Sheltie to the twiggy branches of a nearby bush and carefully stepped forward to check that the hideout was safe.

Sheltie whickered and cocked his head to one side as Emma walked over to the cottage.

She didn't go inside. Emma was

sensible enough to know that old ruins could sometimes fall down. She stood outside and pushed at the first wall with her foot. Nothing happened, so she pushed again. Only this time, she pushed a little harder.

The wall seemed solid enough, so Emma gave it a really hard kick with the sole of her boot.

The *thump* sounded loud, but the wall was solid stone and didn't move.

Emma moved around the cottage, pushing at the walls and leaning her weight against the wooden timbers.

'It's OK, Sheltie, this hideout is quite safe,' she called from behind the tumbledown walls.

That seemed to be enough for the little pony. He stretched his neck and tugged his reins free from their tether. Then he dashed around behind the wall to find Emma.

'Oh!' gasped Emma. 'Sheltie, you gave me such a fright!' She hadn't

expected the little pony to come galloping around the wall like that.

Sheltie blew a loud raspberry which echoed throughout the ruins.

'You see!' exclaimed Emma. 'It's perfectly safe.' And she was right. All the walls were sturdy and solid. The hideout was perfect.

'All it needs is a bit of tidying up and it will be ideal. This is going to be our secret summer den, Sheltie. I can't wait to see Sally's face. She won't believe it when we bring her here!'

The ride home, back to the cottage, didn't seem to take as long as the ride out. And the next morning, when Emma decided to go back and take another look, they covered the distance in no time at all.

'It's not that far, is it, Sheltie?' said Emma.

The little pony pumped his legs quickly as he sniffed the air. Up ahead, they could see the candyfloss tops of the trees, high on the hill, overlooking the secret hideaway.

But suddenly, Sheltie's nostrils flared as he took in a new scent.

'Oh no!' muttered Emma. 'Here comes trouble!'

Chapter Three

Up ahead, Melody Parker was riding
towards them again on Sapphire.

Emma took a deep breath. She
suddenly remembered that Melody
lived on the East Riding. Her father
kept stables. He bred ponies and
offered boarding for horses *and*
ponies. Emma hoped that Melody
would be pleasant again and pass by

without being her usual rude self.

'Hello, Emma,' said Melody. 'That's twice this week. Have you moved to the East Riding?'

Emma said, 'Hello, Melody,' and rode on. Even when Melody Parker was just saying 'hello' she somehow managed to sound nasty.

Emma wondered what Melody was up to, but she didn't look back to see if Melody was watching. She just urged Sheltie on and hoped that they weren't being followed.

They cantered swiftly along the bridle path, then ducked smartly down into the hollow where the secret cottage was hidden.

They paused behind a thick bush

for a few moments, to make sure there was no one around.

Then Emma rode Sheltie right into the cottage, through an opening that would once have been a door. The stone walls of the hideout hid them both from sight.

'This is brilliant, Sheltie,' said Emma. 'Once we're inside, we're invisible!' The little pony looked around at the tumbledown walls and blew a grumbling snort at the ivy dangling above his head.

'It won't take long to tidy up this room,' said Emma. 'Just a few rocks to move and the grass to cut. That's your job, boy.'

Sheltie was brilliant at cropping

grass. The little pony had already discovered the fresh, sweet blades and was busy munching his way through a nice juicy patch.

'I can make some furniture – maybe a table and bench – out of stones and planks of wood,' said Emma. 'And this can be our secret summer hideaway where no one can find us. Sally will love it.'

It took no time at all to move a few rocks and tidy the main room.

Emma then discovered a little stream which trickled its way behind the cottage and bubbled into a small, narrow gully. Beside the stream was a low stone wall.

'Look, Sheltie!' squealed Emma

excitedly. 'Your very own drinking water, fresh from the spring!'

Sheltie lowered his head and drank from the stream. The water was cool and clear. It couldn't have tasted better from his own drinking trough.

Sheltie blew a soft snort of
approval.

'Good!' exclaimed Emma brightly.
'Now I know you think the hideout is
OK.'

Emma piled up some stones and
found planks of wood to make a
comfortable bench and a table.

The main room had a small
window looking out on to the rise of
trees. The window frame and glass
were missing and there was a clear
view of the hill.

Emma sat on her home-made
bench and peered out through the
window. Sheltie stood next to her and
looked too.

Everything was peaceful and quiet

– until Melody Parker came trotting past.

'Oh no!' whispered Emma. She held her breath and watched as Melody and her pony crossed the ridge of candyfloss trees in the distance.

Sheltie also seemed to hold his breath, until suddenly he couldn't hold it any longer and gave a loud belch.

'Shhh!' hissed Emma. She was afraid that Melody would hear. But Melody had already gone and the hideaway was still a secret.

Just then, the sun broke free of the clouds and bathed the hideaway in a brilliant golden light. Sheltie closed his eyes and dozed sleepily in the dappled shade of the wall.

Emma lay on her back in the long grass and looked up at the beautiful blue sky. She wished that Sally could be there too. But she knew that Sally wouldn't be back for nearly a month.

It was soon time to be setting off home, but just as Emma was getting Sheltie ready to leave, the little pony suddenly became very frisky.

'Oh, go on then,' said Emma.

She tucked Sheltie's loose reins through his throat lash, and let him go for a canter. Emma knew that when Sheltie felt frisky it was usually best to let him have a run. In five minutes' time he would be ready to go home. She watched as Sheltie kicked up his heels and gambolled around the outside walls of the hideout.

The ground there was very flat so there was no reason for Emma to worry about Sheltie hurting himself. In fact the ground was *so* flat that Sheltie was able to speed up to a gallop.

Then he decided to try a jump. The low stone wall by the stream jutted out a little way and ran across his path.

It was only a small wall and Sheltie could easily have jumped clean over it. But for some reason he jumped up on to it instead.

Emma gasped as Sheltie's hoofs clattered on the loose stones. Then she screamed as the wall started to collapse and crumble beneath his

weight. The little pony fell
awkwardly. And the stone wall fell
on top of him, trapping his hind legs.

Chapter Four

Poor Sheltie lay on his side. He raised his head and called to Emma with a pitiful whinny.

Emma raced as fast as she could to try and help him. But there was nothing she could do. A whole section of the wall lay across Sheltie's legs, pinning him to the ground. And the stones were far too heavy for

Emma to move on her own.

Emma saw blood on the stones and knew that her little pony was badly hurt.

'Oh, Sheltie!' she cried. 'What shall I do?'

Sheltie gave an unhappy snort. Emma needed to find help quickly. But where? It was a long way back to the village on foot and there didn't seem to be anyone else about. The last cottage they had passed was Mrs Warner's, way back where the downs met the moor. It would take Emma ages to run that far, and Sheltie needed help *now*.

Emma felt like bursting into tears. But she decided she had to be strong. Sheltie was in peril and she needed to concentrate on what to do.

Suddenly Emma heard a familiar sound. It was a pony whickering – the happy noise a pony makes when it blows air through its lips. And it was coming from beyond the candyfloss trees on the ridge above the hideaway.

'Melody Parker,' gasped Emma. She had forgotten about seeing Melody on the hills.

Now she jumped up and ran up the shallow basin slope, waving her arms, calling, 'Melody, Melody. Over here. I need help!'

Emma scrambled up the slope of the hollow and burst out through a mass of ferns, just as Sapphire stepped out from the clump of trees on to the bridle path.

Sapphire hopped sideways, startled by Emma's sudden appearance.

'Whoa! Steady, boy,' yelled Melody.

Then she saw Emma standing in front of them and glared coldly at her.

'Sorry,' said Emma breathlessly, before Melody had a chance to complain. 'I didn't mean to scare Sapphire, but I had to stop you.'

Then she blurted out the whole story while Melody sat and listened.

'You've got to help us,' pleaded Emma. 'You've really got to.'

Emma's heart was banging in her chest and a horrible knot was twisting away inside her stomach. Melody just *had* to help her.

'Come on then,' said Melody. 'Let's go and look at Sheltie.'

She rode her pony down into the hollow with Emma running along closely behind. Emma wanted Melody to ride for help, but Melody insisted on seeing Sheltie first.

The little Shetland pony lay quite

still as Melody rode up. Sheltie peered up at Sapphire through his shaggy forelock and blinked his eyes slowly.

'I think he might be in shock,' said Melody, leaping from the saddle.

Emma knelt down next to Sheltie and stroked his fuzzy face. Then she burst into tears.

'Don't start crying now,' said Melody. 'We've got to try and get this lot off him. I've got a rope in my saddlebag.'

'No!' said Emma. She wiped her face with her sleeve. 'There's blood, and that means Sheltie's legs are cut. The wall's so heavy, we might make things worse if we try to move it.'

'You're right!' agreed Melody. 'I'll race back home and get Dad and Uncle Donny to come out with a horsebox. They know all about ponies.'

She leapt back into the saddle and took off at a mad gallop to fetch help.

'Keep talking to Sheltie,' she yelled

back from the rise. 'Let him hear your voice. I won't be long.'

Then she disappeared in a thunder of drumming hoofs, leaving Emma and Sheltie alone.

Chapter Five

Emma knelt down next to Sheltie and brushed his forelock away from his eyes.

'It won't be long, boy,' soothed Emma. 'Melody and Sapphire have gone to fetch help. We'll soon have you out of here.'

Sheltie's eyes flickered and he managed a soft snort.

Emma wished she could soothe Sheltie's legs beneath the wall that trapped him, but she knew she couldn't move the stones. Emma hated the thought that her pony was suffering.

Emma looked at her watch. Melody had only been gone two minutes, yet it seemed like an hour.

'Just hang on, Sheltie,' Emma said. 'Help will be here soon!'

The little Shetland pony lay quite still. His sides heaved with each breath he took and he whimpered through trembling lips as he tried to raise his head.

'Please be strong,' Emma whispered.

Emma was being as brave as she knew how. She loved Sheltie more than anything in the whole world, but she couldn't do anything to help him.

She looked at her watch again. Five minutes. *Oh! Please hurry, Melody. PLEASE!* she thought.

Emma whispered comforting words into Sheltie's velvet ears and stroked his soft furry face. 'It won't be long now,' she murmured.

Fifteen minutes passed before Emma heard the sound of an engine struggling up the rise beyond the woods.

She stood up and looked towards the candyfloss trees. Emma could see

45

a green Land Rover pulling a horsebox out into the sunshine.

Melody was riding behind on Sapphire, and waved to Emma, who was standing below in the hollow.

'Quickly, quickly!' yelled Emma.

The Land Rover swung left and slowly rolled down the gentle slope, rumbling across the grass with the horsebox behind.

It pulled to a halt and two men jumped out. One of them had dark hair and was about the same age as Emma's dad.

'Hello, I'm Melody's father,' he said. 'And this is Uncle Donny. He knows all about ponies.'

Uncle Donny was a bit older, with

silver-white hair and a matching silver beard.

Emma had never been so pleased to see anyone in all her life.

Melody and Sapphire followed Emma and the two men behind the hideout to where Sheltie was trapped.

Mr Parker quickly checked Sheltie over and immediately set to work on a rescue plan with Uncle Donny. The two men tied rope to bits of the broken wall and used the Land Rover to pull the heavy stones off Sheltie's legs.

The little pony whinnied in pain as the heavy wall was pulled aside to set him free.

Mr Parker examined Sheltie's legs.
'It doesn't look good,' he said.

Then Uncle Donny took a look. He
stroked Sheltie's face and felt the

length of his legs from rump to hoof.
But he said nothing.

Emma watched and listened with
her heart beating hard against her
ribs. Melody stayed back with
Sapphire and remained silent.

'I think we should get Sheltie back
to his paddock,' said Mr Parker at
last. 'But I don't think he has much of
a chance.'

'What!' Emma almost screamed.

'It's his left hind leg,' said Mr
Parker. 'I think it's broken. And a
pony with a broken leg is better off
when it's dealt with kindly.'

'What do you mean?' asked Emma.
'Of course I'll be kind to Sheltie.'

Mr Parker tried to explain that

when a pony has a broken leg, it
usually means that the pony doesn't
survive.

'No!' screamed Emma. 'He has to
survive, he *has* to!'

Uncle Donny tried to calm Emma down.

'I think there *is* something we can do for Sheltie,' he told her. 'But we must let the vet take a look at him first.'

Chapter Six

Mr Parker managed to back the
horsebox right up to where Sheltie
was lying. Uncle Donny strapped
a splint to Sheltie's leg and the
little pony was able to hobble, with
a lot of help, into the waiting
horsebox.

'I think we had better get Sheltie
home,' he said. 'This little fellow

needs a visit from the vet right away!'

Emma sat in-between the two men and wished they could drive faster. Melody trotted Sapphire alongside and smiled kindly at Emma through the car window.

It seemed really odd to be friendly with Melody after all the times Melody had been nasty. But today she had been brilliant. Melody had raced off and brought back help just as quickly as she could.

As the car and horsebox pulled up outside the cottage, Sheltie blew a very loud, snorting whinny. Mum and Dad came running down the garden path to see what was happening. They could hear Sheltie calling from inside the horsebox and knew immediately that something was wrong.

Emma leapt from the Land Rover and ran up to Mum.

'It's Sheltie,' she blurted. 'There's been an accident and we think he's broken his leg!'

Mum gave Emma a big cuddle and held her close. She smoothed Emma's hair and gently brushed the tears from her eyes.

'I'd better phone the vet straight away,' said Dad. 'It sounds as though Sheltie is in real trouble.'

Mr Parker and Uncle Donny

managed to get Sheltie into his field
shelter. They made the little pony
comfortable and waited for the vet to
arrive.

Melody was very quiet. She stayed
in Sheltie's paddock with Sapphire

and looked very upset. Everyone was really worried about Sheltie.

Mr Thorne, the vet, had looked after the little pony many times before. When he had finished examining him, he looked very serious.

'Sheltie has fractured his leg,' said the vet. 'A broken leg is a serious problem for a pony.' Mr Thorne looked very sad. 'The only kind thing to do when a pony has fractured its leg is to put it to sleep and save the pony from a lot of suffering.'

Emma was horrified. 'No!' she cried.

'Sometimes,' said Mum sadly, 'a pony is so badly injured that the best thing to do is to be kind. And saying goodbye is sometimes the only thing to do.'

'But I can't say goodbye to Sheltie,' pleaded Emma. 'I just can't. *People* break their legs and get better all the time.'

'But ponies are different,' said Mum. 'A broken leg is very bad for a pony.'

'But Sheltie is *different*,' sobbed Emma. 'He *must* get better! I can't let him go.'

Emma collapsed in a flood of tears. Dad gave her a cuddle and she noticed that he was crying too.

'I'm sorry, darling,' he said. 'But I think it's the only way.'

'No, it's not,' Uncle Donny
interrupted. 'There *is* another way!'

Mr Thorne looked puzzled.

'An "angel",' said Uncle Donny.
'We could cast the leg in plaster and
support Sheltie in a sling. We call it

an angel, where I come from. And
I've seen it work lots of times before.
My grandfather taught me everything
he knew about angels.'

Mr Thorne looked concerned. 'You
can't be sure it will work,' he said.

Mum looked at Emma. 'It's worth a
try,' she said.

'Oh, please, please try,' sobbed
Emma. 'I can't lose Sheltie. I just
can't.'

'All right,' said the vet. 'If that's
what you want to do!'

'It *is* worth a try,' agreed Dad.

'Please,' said Emma.

Melody slipped from Sapphire's
saddle and whispered to Emma,
'Uncle Donny has made miracles

happen with the angel before. I bet
he can help Sheltie!'

Melody didn't seem so awful any
more. She was acting like a real
friend. And right now Sheltie needed
all the friends he could get.

Chapter Seven

Melody's father and Uncle Donny
went back to their stables to collect
all the things they needed to make
the angel.

Mr Thorne gave Sheltie a pain-
killing injection and an antibiotic.
Then he dressed the cuts and set
Sheltie's broken leg in a plaster cast.

The little pony couldn't stand

properly on his own and was lying quietly on his side. Emma knelt in the fresh straw next to him and lightly touched the bandages on his legs. She wished that she could somehow magic all the pain away and make Sheltie's broken leg as good as new.

The little pony gave a long sigh and closed his eyes.

'I've given him a tranquillizer to help him sleep,' said the vet. 'Poor Sheltie's had a terrible shock.'

'Some ponies and horses die from shock,' said Melody. Emma could tell she didn't mean to be unkind. It was the truth. 'You have to stay with them all the time and talk to them,' she continued. 'Uncle Donny says that they like to hear voices. It helps them to get better.'

Mr Thorne nodded. Melody was right.

'Then I want to stay with Sheltie all the time,' Emma decided. 'I want to stay with him here in the shelter and sleep here too! Can I, Mum? Please? Can I bring my sleeping bag out here and sleep with Sheltie?'

Mum gave Emma an understanding look. She knew that Emma would stay in the shelter anyway, even if she said no.

'Of course you can,' said Mum, smiling.

Emma felt relieved. She was being

very brave, and being with Sheltie
would help *her* too.

It was the middle of summer and
the nights were warm and balmy.
Emma would be safe and comfortable
out in the shelter in her sleeping
bag.

'I'll camp out with you, if you like,'
Melody offered.

'Thanks,' said Emma. 'But I'd
really like to be on my own with
Sheltie.'

Melody looked hurt.

'It was nice of you to offer,' Mum
told her. 'And thank you for bringing
your father and uncle to help.'

Melody brightened up a bit.

'Yes, thank you,' said Emma. 'I'm

really glad you came along when you did.'

Just then, Sheltie gave a soft snort in his sleep.

'It's all right,' soothed Emma. She stroked the little pony's face. 'I'm here. And I won't be going anywhere. I'll be here with you.'

Mr Parker and Uncle Donny came back with the angel.

It didn't look much like an angel, thought Emma, when she saw it lying on the ground. It looked like a big canvas sling.

Everyone watched as Uncle Donny fixed the angel in place. It hung from the rafters in Sheltie's field shelter, and supported the little pony under his tummy. Now Emma could see how the sling got its name.

'It makes Sheltie look as if he's got big white wings,' said Emma. 'Just like an angel!'

'Look how it keeps Sheltie's feet just touching the ground,' said Dad.

'The angel will keep the weight off Sheltie's injured leg,' Uncle Donny told Emma.

'And that might help it mend,' added the vet.

'Sheltie *will* get better, won't he? I just know he will!' said Emma.

'Let's hope so,' Mum sighed.

Emma looked at Sheltie. He was half asleep, hanging from the angel. The canvas sling was tucked under

Sheltie's belly, keeping his broken leg comfortably off the ground.

Emma planted a kiss on Sheltie's soft muzzle and told him how much

she loved him. The little pony harrumphed, then he sneezed and drifted deeper into sleep.

There was nothing else they could do. Mr Thorne had more calls to make, and Mr Parker and Uncle Donny went home. Melody and Sapphire left too.

Mum helped Emma with her sleeping bag while Dad fixed up a special heat lamp to his old car battery. Although it was summer, the evenings could sometimes get chilly. The lamp would keep the field shelter warm and cosy.

That night, before Emma went to bed, she made a bran mash for Sheltie, and fed him by hand with a spoon. Her sleeping bag lay snuggled amongst the straw in the far corner of the shelter. Dad had also rigged up a buzzer so that Emma could call him in the cottage at any time during the night.

'It's just you and me, Sheltie,' whispered Emma.

She hung her arms gently around the little pony's neck and gave him a loving hug.

'I'll be here all the time,' said Emma. 'I won't leave you alone for a minute.'

Sheltie flicked his eyes and blew a soft snort.

'You're a fighter, aren't you, boy?' said Emma. 'You won't give up, will

Chapter Eight

The next two weeks were awful.
Emma spent every day in the shelter
with Sheltie. She talked to him all the
time and hoped for a miracle.

But Sheltie didn't seem to be
getting any better at all. He hung
from the angel with his head hanging
low on his chest. His eyes had lost
their sparkle and his mane hung

down the side of his neck in tatty fronds.

Emma stroked Sheltie's furry face and whispered in his ear. She read him stories and told him how much she loved him. But he still looked very sick.

The vet came every day. He examined Sheltie's leg and checked the plaster cast.

Uncle Donny came too. He put his hands on Sheltie's leg and closed his eyes. He told Emma that he was imagining Sheltie's leg getting better.

Then he lowered the angel, just a tiny bit each time, to get Sheltie used to carrying his own weight.

'Is it working?' asked Emma.

Uncle Donny smiled. 'The angel
can only do so much,' he said. 'The
rest is up to Sheltie. And you.'

'*Me*?' exclaimed Emma.

'Yes, *you*,' said Uncle Donny.
'Sheltie needs to know that he *must*
get better for you. Talk to him and

remind him about all the fun you have together.'

Emma did everything that Uncle Donny said. She tried very hard and thought of all the wonderful times she had spent with Sheltie.

She brushed the little pony's coat gently as she talked to him, and smiled as Sheltie whickered softly in her ear.

Every day she wished and hoped that the angel would save Sheltie.

But when Mr Thorne visited, he looked at Sheltie and shook his head. He didn't want the little pony to suffer.

'It might still be kinder if we put Sheltie to sleep,' he told Emma softly.

'It's not fair to keep him if he's in pain.'

Emma closed her eyes. She didn't want to listen to the vet's words. She felt sick. All she wanted to think about was Sheltie getting better and running through the meadows with the wind in his mane.

Mum put her arm around Emma's shoulders.

'If Sheltie can't walk, it would be cruel to keep him,' she said. Her voice was sad but kind. 'And we should listen to Mr Thorne, Emma. I know you love Sheltie. But we must do what's right for *him*.'

'I don't want Sheltie to suffer,' sobbed Emma, 'but I don't want to lose him either.' She felt awful.

'Let's give him one more week,' said Dad. 'Then we shall have to decide.'

The days dragged by slowly. Emma lived with Sheltie in the shelter and hand-fed him at every mealtime.

The little pony seemed happier and had a good appetite. But he was still being held by the angel, barely touching the straw below.

Emma spoke to Sheltie all the time. She read him more stories and sang songs. And at bedtime, when it was warm and cosy in her sleeping bag amongst the straw, she planned rides and adventures until she fell asleep.

Near the end of the third week, the vet, Melody and her father, and Uncle Donny came to see Sheltie again. Mr Thorne cut away the plaster cast. Then Uncle Donny lowered the angel to the floor and Sheltie stood on his own four legs for the first time since the accident.

Emma held her breath and leaned against Mum as Sheltie shuffled uneasily. Then she gasped in horror as he toppled to the ground.

Chapter Nine

'Don't worry,' said Uncle Donny.
'There's plenty of straw down on the floor.'

Sheltie rolled on to his side and Emma went to help him.

'No!' said Uncle Donny softly.
'Leave him be. Let him do it by himself.'

Mum put her arms around Emma

and held her close.

'Come on, Sheltie! You can do it,'
Emma said. She bit her bottom lip
and waited.

'He's bound to be a bit wobbly at
first,' said Uncle Donny.

Mr Thorne was there too, watching
carefully. 'If the bone hasn't knitted
together properly, I'll have to do
something,' he warned. 'We can't just
stand here and watch Sheltie suffer. It
wouldn't be fair.'

Emma knew exactly what the vet
meant. She didn't want to lose
Sheltie, but she couldn't bear to think
of him suffering either.

The little pony looked at Emma
and whinnied as he rocked himself

up and tried to stand. But again he tottered and fell.

This time Emma pulled away from Mum and went to hug Sheltie with tears flooding down her cheeks.

'He wants me to help,' she said. 'I know he does.'

'Emma might be right,' said Mr Parker.

'You can do it, can't you, boy?' Emma said. She stroked Sheltie's neck and talked to him.

'Come on, boy. I know you feel wobbly, but you can make it.' She gave him a hug and her salty tears trickled on to his face.

The little pony rolled up on to his legs again.

'That's it, boy. Nice and steady,' encouraged Emma.

Sheltie's legs were trembling and he looked very shaky. But at last, he

stood on his own. And this time he didn't fall.

'Yes,' said Emma excitedly. 'Yes!' She put her arms gently around Sheltie's neck and buried her face in his mane.

Mr Thorne stepped forward to examine Sheltie. He ran his hands over the little pony's injured leg.

'The bone seems to have knitted perfectly,' he said with a big smile.

'The angel has never failed me yet,' said Uncle Donny with a grin. He ruffled Sheltie's forelock and the little pony nudged his hand and gave it a lick. Then he blew a very loud raspberry.

'We haven't heard one of those for

ages,' laughed Emma. Then she gave Uncle Donny a big hug too.

Everyone was relieved that Sheltie's leg was mended.

'He'll still need to rest up for several weeks,' said Mr Thorne. 'Gentle exercise and walks only. You won't be able to ride him for a while.'

Emma smiled. She knew exactly how to take care of Sheltie. She had the rest of the summer holidays to spend nursing him back to health.

'I don't know how to thank you enough,' said Dad to Uncle Donny.

'Seeing Emma smiling again was enough,' replied Uncle Donny. 'But there is just *one* small thing I'm going to ask Emma to do for me.'

After Mr Thorne had shown Emma
how to wrap a support bandage
around Sheltie's injured leg, Uncle
Donny took her to one side.

'It's about Melody,' he began.
'She's got no friends of her own and
isn't very happy at school. I know
she sometimes makes trouble, but
that's because no one bothers with
her. She's not *all* bad when you get to
know her. Do you think you could
try and be friends? What do you
think?'

'Well, we both love ponies,' said
Emma. 'So that will be a start!'

Melody was standing with
Sapphire by the paddock fence, so
Emma wandered over.

'Mr Thorne says Sheltie's going to be fine,' Emma told her.

Melody looked a little bit sad. 'It would have been awful if you'd lost him,' she said. 'Sheltie's your best friend, isn't he?'

Emma nodded and swallowed the

lump in her throat. 'I want to really, really thank you for helping us,' she told Melody.

Melody looked embarrassed. 'Oh, it was nothing,' she mumbled. 'That's what friends are for.'

Emma grinned.

'We can be friends, can't we?' Melody asked.

'Of course we can,' said Emma. 'Now, tell me all about the new foal at your stables! Uncle Donny said it's only a few days old.'

Melody smiled. 'You can come and see him if you like,' she said brightly.

A week later, Sally came back from her holiday in Scotland. The first thing she did when she got home was to phone Emma.

'Hello,' said Sally, when Emma picked up the phone. 'What's been happening in Little Applewood while I've been away?'

'Oh, lots of things,' said Emma. 'I'll tell you all about it tomorrow when we go over to Melody's to see the new foal at the stables.'

For a moment there was silence.

'Melody's?' asked Sally, sounding as if she could hardly believe her ears.

'Melody Parker,' said Emma. 'She can't wait to show you their new foal, Bramble. And we want to show you our new secret hideout too.

Melody's been talking about it for days.'

Sally laughed. It was obvious that quite a lot had happened while she had been away.

And Emma couldn't wait to tell her all about it.

If you like making friends, fun, excitement and adventure, then you'll love

The little pony with the big heart!

Sheltie is the lovable little Shetland pony with a big personality. He is cheeky, full of fun and has a heart of gold. His owner, Emma, knew that she and Sheltie would be best friends as soon as she saw him. She could tell that he thought so too by the way his brown eyes twinkled beneath his big, bushy mane. When Emma, her mum and dad and little brother, Joshua, first moved to Little Applewood, she thought that she might not like living there. But life is never dull with Sheltie around. He is full of mischief and he and Emma have lots of exciting adventures together.

Share Sheltie and Emma's adventures in:

SHELTIE THE SHETLAND PONY
SHELTIE SAVES THE DAY
SHELTIE AND THE RUNAWAY
SHELTIE FINDS A FRIEND
SHELTIE TO THE RESCUE
SHELTIE IN DANGER

Sheltie™

to the Rescue

The little pony with the big heart!

Emma thinks that going to Summerland Bay
will be the best holiday ever – especially as
Sheltie can come too. Emma can't believe it
when she sees snobby Alice Parker. She is
always making fun of Sheltie. But when Alice
and her pony get into trouble, Sheltie is the
only one who can save them.

READ MORE IN PUFFIN

For children of all ages, Puffin represents quality and variety – the very best in publishing today around the world.

For complete information about books available from Puffin – and Penguin – and how to order them, contact us at the appropriate address below. Please note that for copyright reasons the selection of books varies from country to country.

On the World Wide Web: www.penguin.co.uk

In the United Kingdom: Please write to *Dept. EP, Penguin Books Ltd, Bath Road, Harmondsworth, West Drayton, Middlesex UB7 0DA*

In the United States: Please write to *Penguin Putnam inc., P.O. Box 12289, Dept B, Newark, New Jersey 07101-5289* or call 1-800-788-6262

In Canada: Please write to *Penguin Books Canada Ltd, 10 Alcorn Avenue, Suite 300, Toronto, Ontario M4V 3B2*

In Australia: Please write to *Penguin Books Australia Ltd, P.O. Box 257, Ringwood, Victoria 3134*

In New Zealand: Please write to *Penguin Books (NZ) Ltd, Private Bag 102902, North Shore Mail Centre, Auckland 10*

In India: Please write to *Penguin Books India Pvt Ltd, 11 Panscheel Shopping Centre, Panscheel Park, New Delhi 110 017*

In the Netherlands: Please write to *Penguin Books Netherlands bv, Postbus 3507, NL-1001 AH Amsterdam*

In Germany: Please write to *Penguin Books Deutschland GmbH, Metzlerstrasse 26, 60594 Frankfurt am Main*

In Spain: Please write to *Penguin Books S. A., Bravo Murillo 19, 1º B, 28015 Madrid*

In Italy: Please write to *Penguin Italia s.r.l., Via Felice Casati 20, I-20124 Milano*

In France: Please write to *Penguin France S. A., 17 rue Lejeune, F-31000 Toulouse*